animals

New and Collected Micro Stories and Flash Fiction

by Paul Rogalus

Published by Human Error Publishing

www.humanerrorpublishing.com
paul@humanerrorpublishing.com

ISBN: 978-1-948521-13-0

Original cover art by
Charles Kuizinas, of Cosmic Moose Art

Acknowledgments:

The following stories have been previously published:

"Early 80's Boston: The End of the World": Crystal Drum
"Lesarde" and "Flies": Babel Magazine
"The Exploding Man": Nerve Cowboy
"The Stump": Flashshot
"Border Patrol": The Bukowski Hangover Project
"Snake Charmer": Sleet
"Transformer Man": WEIRDYEAR
"Hunter Thompson's Ashes": Drunk Monkeys
"Giant Rat" and "Johnny Fist": Burningword
"Looking for Jack Kerouac's Grave": Flashquake
"Visions of Ben": The Drexel Online Journal
"The GoodTime Bar": Dogzplot
"Ship of Fools": Microfiction Monday
"Grateful Black Denim" and
"The Beat Poets": Flash Fiction Magazine
"The Giant": Full of Crow
"Big Margaret": Friday Flash Fiction

For Jess and Mark

Table of Contents

Part I: "a soul too big for a body"

Part II: "Electrified Skeletons"

Part III: "Meat Sculptures"

Part I:
"a soul too big for a body"

The Giant

There was this massive guy in McGarry's Tavern—just freakishly huge, like six foot ten, with scraggily Neil Young hair and big old army jacket—making him look a little bit like Chief Bromden in One Flew Over the Cuckoo's Nest. This guy drew a lot of attention in the bar. You could tell some people were thinking this giant guy would be trouble.

A woman I knew said she'd seen this guy before in a near -by town, wearing a giant dress—but I didn't really believe her—because, well, this woman was always just saying shit. I looked over at him and I saw that the giant was drinking a White Russian—just like the Dude in The Big Lebowski— and somehow I knew that this guy was not going to cause trouble.

The band broke into a serious reggae version of "Fire on the Mountain" by the Grateful Dead—and so I got up to dance— because I always dance whenever I hear the Dead—well, I sort of dance, but mostly I just sort of sway in slow motion. Next thing I know the giant is dancing next to me—in this lumbering but graceful sort of manner. So, in a way, I danced with the giant. When the song ended the giant nodded to me—in a Dudely sort of way—and then he just lumbered off.

And so, three days later, when I saw the giant on the channel nine news—having been arrested for assaulting a police officer with extreme violence—I knew—deep down in my soul— that it wasn't true . . . that the officer had just been intimidated by this freaky giant—just as I'd been—before I danced with him.

Big Margaret

Big Big Margaret—enormous gray-haired woman—in a loose-fitting purple tye-dyed dress, nodding to the live music in the bar. She wants to dance sooooooo bad, as the three-man jam band breaks into "Fire—fire on the mountain." And Margaret just starts swaying— while still sitting at her table, not quite dancing—but moving—grooving—oozing funkiness.

And with her eyes--she's dancing—with anyone in the bar who will meet her gaze.
And then, when someone smiles back--well, that's a good night. Yeah, that's what we all live for.
Margaret.

Grateful Black Denim

My brother Mark died the same year Jerry Garcia died, 1995. The only belonging of Mark's that I have is a black denim winter coat that he'd just bought and only worn a few times. His wife gave it to me, since we were about the same size. I couldn't wear the coat for a few years. I mean—it was my brother's—and he was dead. But—I played Jerry Garcia music—more than ever.

Then, one winter I wore Mark's black denim coat to snow-blow the driveway. After that, I wore it every time I did the driveway. A sort of ritual. My brother helped me get through the winter.

And now, the black denim winter coat is really beat to shit worn out, with white stuffing bulging out of the sleeves. But I can't throw it out—I can't stop wearing it—it was my brother's. My last physical connection to him.

So lately I think about my brother Mark when I hear certain Grateful Dead songs, like "He's Gone." " . . . gone, gone, nothin's gonna bring him back." Mark never really liked the Grateful Dead, as far as I know, but still—Mark and Jerry— they died together—in my mind. In my soul. My two brothers. Brothers in arms—worn out arms with stuffing bulging out of a worn out denim coat—like a soul too big for a body.

Jack O' Lanterns

The October when I was 20, I was living in a rented house in Bay Shores with three art majors, who were also serious stoners. The night before Halloween we noticed that the pumpkins on the front steps of most of our neighbors' houses had not yet been carved into jack o' lanterns. We thought that was sad—and so we went out late at night and kidnapped the neighborhood pumpkins—and brought them to our house— where we worked for hours, deep into the early morning, listening to Pink Floyd and carving fantastic, very elaborate jack o' lanterns, with wild, beautiful, funky faces. And then we went back around the neighborhood and put them all back onto their home steps.

And the next day we walked around our neighborhood— and listened—as a couple kids found their jack o' lanterns— ex- cited, asking their father if the Great Pumpkin had made their jack o' lanterns. The father shrugged and said he guessed so. And so we walked home, feeling noble, feeling like we were saving humanity—with ART. And then, after we got home, we realized that one of our neighbors had called the police on us. Humanity was still doomed.

"Beat Poets"

"I saw the best minds of my generation destroyed by mad-ness---" Ben screaming out the back of Steve's Oldsmobile as it bombs around Harvard Square in search of Club 47—where Allen Ginsberg, Gregory Corso, and Peter Orlovsky are doing a reading—the Beat poets—our heroes—friends of Jack Kerouac's. The Beat poets—the reason we love poetry.

There's a huge line, more than a block long, in front of Club 47—and by the time we get to the door the show is sold out. "They'll be doing a second show at 9:30," the door man tells us. "You mean, like Wayne Newton in Las Vegas," Steve's girlfriend Scarlette asks him. Ben just starts to scream—like a wild animal—a loud, painful, primordial scream—and the manager comes out and asks the doorman if he should call the police. "We ARE the police," Steve tells him.

We decide to wait in a bar for the 9:30 show, but Ben doesn't want to wait—he wants to find a back entrance to Club 47—to sneak in and explore. He hops over an iron fence and calls us over, saying he found a way in. So, we follow him.

Ben looks through a window—and sees Ginsberg on stage—right in front of him—and Ben starts to scream: "I am the ghost of Walt Whitman! I have come to shoot forth filaments from my soul, filaments from my subconscious, filaments from my asshole!"

Ginsberg turns around, confused. Steve pulls a bottle of Mad Dog out of his coat, and swigs.

Scarlette finds an unlocked door, and we head in, reeling lost down a dark hallway, trying random doors. We stumble into a sort of dressing room—with a few tables and old padded chairs. We explore. There are old coats and satchel bags—a table with bottled water, a bottle of wine, a platter of cheese and crackers. We sit down. Ben puts on an old overcoat that he finds—and wonders out loud if it's Allen

Ginsberg's coat. Scarlette shrugs and says, "Maybe so."
She tries on another overcoat she finds on a chair. "Maybe
Kerouac borrowed this coat sometime—maybe Neil Cassidy
wore it." Steve takes a long slug of wine and passes me the
bottle. I take a swig—just as Allen Ginsberg, Gregory Corso,
and Peter Orlovsky walk into the room. We all freeze.

  They're looking old, the Beat poets—worn down, faded.
They're looking beat. Ginsberg starts to stammer: "But, but,
but those are OUR chairs, and, and those are OUR coats."
He's a babbling old man.

  Gregory Corso—wild-eyed, with a messy mop of graying
hair—takes in the scene—and then he starts to laugh—a
big, booming, crazy laugh—his mouth wide open—exposing
spaces from missing teeth. Scarlette quickly takes off the
overcoat she's wearing—I put the wine back onto the table—
and we hustle out of the room, as Ginsberg keeps stammer-
ing excitedly about us being there, and Ben drops the coat
he's been wearing in a chair by the door.

  Back in the dark hallway, we get lost again—and we end up
in the kitchen. We see a door to the outside and hurry toward
it, but the manager grabs Ben by the shoulder and says: "Hey,
aren't you the boy that screamed?" Silence for a moment.
And then Ben bellows out his booming laugh. He shakes
his shoulder free from the manager and he screams out:
"Gregory Corso has no teeth!"

  We hurry off into the Boston night—looking for a cheap bar,
Ben still hollering: "I am the boy that screamed." He laughs,
louder, and louder, as we ramble on—looking for action—
looking for NEW Beat poets.

"Crazy - Funny"

The first time I met Katrina, she was in the check-out line in a liquor store in Connecticut—and she was either pretending that she was from a foreign country and that she didn't understand English—or that she was deaf. She smiled innocently at the cashier and she dumped a big pile of change down on the counter—and then every time he asked her a question she just shook her head, dumbfounded. He ended up counting out all of her change for her and even giving her 80 cents off on a bottle of rum—just to get rid of her. I knew I had to meet her—and so I talked to her at her car in the parking lot, complimenting her on her act. And then I asked her out.

The first time we went out, Katrina drove. She just really wanted to drive. We were on our way to a movie and she just stopped her car in the middle of a fairly busy street— and she got out and went and knelt down in front of the car, looking down at the pavement. A few other cars stopped— and people came over to see what was wrong—to see why she had stopped her car to look at the street. Deadpan, she looked up at an older gentleman and said, "It's these damn ants. They take sooo long to cross the road." The older gentleman shook his head and walked away swearing under his breath, calling her crazy. Yeah, she was crazy, I thought. But crazy-funny.

It was just after the first snowfall of the season when we went out again. And I drove this time. I didn't have an ice scraper for my windshield, so I took the metal spatula that my father used for grilling to get the ice off—and I just threw the spatula in the back seat.

We went to a bar and listened to some folk singers for a while—and then we decided to leave—and drive to the other side of the parking lot—and park. We were making out, and Katrina was pretty aggressive—and so there was much fondling and unzipping of zippers—and then all of a sudden there was a police officer tapping on my window with a flashlight, and then shining it in my face. Shit. I rolled down the window.

"Can I help you, officer?"

"What's the knife for?" he asked me.
"The what?"

"The knife in the backseat." He shined his flashlight beam onto the barbecue spatula in the backseat.

"Oh, no, officer, that's not a knife, that's a spatula—I was using it to clear the ice on my windshield."

He swung the flashlight beam to Katrina.

"Are you alright, ma'am," he asked.

Katrina jumped right into another crazy-funny character. "This man kidnapped me, officer. And now he's forcing me to have sex with him."

My eyes popped out, and I came very close to shitting my pants.

When the cop told me to "step out of the car," it was Katrina who popped out, lightning- quick—laughing a twisted sort of cackle.

She hopped around the front of the car over to the cop, saying, "No, just kidding, officer. I'm the one that really wants to have sex—he's a little slow, if you ask me." And then, without missing a beat, she asked the cop, "Hey, can I see your gun? Just, you know, hold it? Maybe spin it around? Oh, and the hat too. Pretty please?" She lurched to grab the policeman's hat, but he dodged out of her grasp.

The cop was very confused, and so he let us go, just to get rid of us. And I was very confused, and very scared, so I took Katrina home.

I never called her again—and I never saw her again. She just scared me a little too much.

It's been quite a few years, but sometimes when I'm back in my hometown in Connecticut, I just kind of look around for her, like when I go to a liquor store. And every once in a while, I think I hear Katrina's twisted, crazy-funny laugh—and just for a split second I feel like I'm going to shit my pants. She had a power over me. Maybe she still does. I miss her.

King Rex

When I was seventeen, I worked at the Rockville Shell station—a 24 hour, full service gas station right off the highway. When I was hired they gave me a couple of station workshirts with name patches sewn on the fronts of them that said "Rex." They'd been ordered for the guy whose place I was taking. Apparently Rex was a pretty big guy.

The shirts were given to me by a mechanic named Lenny, a chain-smoking, whiskey-voiced guy with a thick mustache, who kind of looked like Al Pacino. I looked at the name tags and said: "Rex means 'king' in Latin."
Lenny looked at me through a cloud of cigarette smoke and said: "The fuck're you talkin' about?"

So, I started to call myself Rex at work—and with my customers—and I made up a background for my new Rex identity, a very elaborate background: my brother Earl had been killed in Vietnam; I had my own pro-stock race car that I'd built myself, and that I raced at Connecticut Dragway; I hunted dangerous animals with a crossbow; and I could fix anything on a car.

In reality, all of the details I'd made up for "Rex's" identity were the polar opposite of my own. And I really didn't know jack shit about cars. So, the first time I was working alone on the late night graveyard shift, and a car came in with a problem—leaking some kind of fluid—I just wrapped up the leaking hose with a lot of duct tape—and I charged them twenty dollars. And then I watched the car drive back onto the highway—as more and more smoke started to spew out from under the hood.

And I was pretty sure that I wouldn't be playing the part of King Rex for very much longer.

Hemingway and Steve

In a bar with Ernest Hemingway and my friend Steve—as usual Steve is dressed all in black, and wearing sunglasses. He tells me about the guy who sits at the desk next to him at work.

"Big, fat, greasy man with slicked back black hair and plastic shoes," Steve says. He's always sniffling. Always. Wiping wet snot on the sleeve of his sports coat."

Hemingway, as usual, needs attention and has to interrupt: "You know, Fitzgerald had a very small penis—it bothered him a great deal—mainly because of that bitch Zelda." Steve shakes his head and looks away, drinking his beer. He's always been a little annoyed by Hemingway. Hemingway goes on: "My penis is somewhat larger than average in size, and it's very wide." He looks at me for a reaction. I shrug.
"Tremendously wide," he goes on.

I look back at Steve. "So, Ronnie told me you guys might be getting your band back together."

"Yeah, why not," Steve says. "He's got a few gigs lined up for us, decent money."

Hemingway is intrigued. "So, you play in a rock band. What is the name of your band?"

"Criminalingo," Steve says. "We used to be called 'Living with the Bomb,' but then we had to change it because there was already another band called 'Living with the Bomb,' and they had the rights to it."

"Living with the Bomb," Hemingway says. "I like that. You should have kept that one."

"It was a legal issue," I explain.

Hemingway shakes his head. "Doesn't matter. You should have stood your ground. You should have fought for the name. Like a man."

Steve calls Hemingway a dickhead.

Hemingway challenges Steve to an arm wrestling match. Steve says no, he doesn't want to. Hemingway snorts, and mumbles "coward" under his breath.

Steve stares at Hemingway for a moment. "I know," he says. "Let's play mumbly peg."

"Mumbly peg, what's that?" Hemingway asks.

Steve pulls a large switchblade knife out of his pocket, and flicks it open. "Mumbly peg," he says, "also known as 'five finger filet,' is a game in which you take a knife and stab the table between all of your fingers as fast as you possibly can."

Steve then puts his hand on the bar, palm down, fingers spread widely, and very rapidly jabs the knife into the bar wood in between all of his fingers in a rhythmic pattern.

Hemingway's eyes light up. "Jesus Christ," he blurts out, slapping Steve on the shoulder. "I'll give you that round, all right. Good show. Barkeep, get this man a drink, on me."

The salty looking bartender limps over. "Yeah, o.k. . . . but Steve, you gotta stop stabbing the shit outa my bar like that." As the bartender goes to get the beer, Hunter Thompson suddenly appears at Steve's side, in his aviator sunglasses and cigarette holder, very excited, gesticulating wildly.

"Good god, man, are you playing mumbly peg? I'm in, man, I'm in. I want next game."

"Downtown Train"

Maggie and I went to see a Tom Waits tribute band at a bar in Laconia—and the two of us were the only ones there. Nice guys. They played a song from "Small Change" that I really liked, so I cheered pretty loud—and the bass player said, "Thanks, Matt." We were important to them—they had us outnumbered. Another couple came in partway through their second set—a really drunk middle aged woman and a really, really skinny guy—but he passed out after a song or two—fell flat on the floor like something from a Road Runner cartoon. Middle aged woman dragged him away, calling him a "pussy."

The guys in the band dedicated the next song to him— "Downtown Train"—"for the passed out guy being dragged out of the bar."

Brockton Girls

The dirty-blonde tough girls hang out—smoking cigarettes on the front porch of the big old white house next to the Polish church. Greasy, worn-out jeans. Scuffed leather boots. Loud rock music blaring—Allman Brothers—Lynard Skynard—"Nuthin' Fancy." Freeee Bird! Raw music. The Brockton girls—from the old part of town. Old mill-town Brocton. The wild girls

I went to a party at the old white house once when I was seventeen. The Romanowski's lived there back then. That was my first Brocton girl party. The Romanowski's house smelled like cabbage and kielbasa—and sweat. I remember Lynard Skynard blaring on the stereo. "Free Bird." Cases of Pabst Blue Ribbon talls stacked in the kitchen. Leather-jacketed hoods I'd seen in the school parking lot—playing quarters at the kitchen table. Rolling joints. Doing shots of Jim Beam. And making me do shots with them. Then—Mary Ann Romanowski grabbing my hand and pulling me into the back yard—telling me it was her birthday—and that she wanted a birthday kiss. Smiling—with big, wild, flashing eyes, hungry eyes. Pulling me toward her—her breath tasting like summer. Her eyes burning down into mine and I put my arms around her, with Bruce Springsteen now ripping out of the open kitchen window: "Baby this town rips the bones from your back." Mary Ann smiling, holding me, screaming along with Bruce, "It's a death trap, It's a suicide rap. We gotta get out while we're young." Her eyes searching. The night sky.
Desire. Life.

The dirty-blonde Brockton girls are dancing to country rock on the porch of the big white house. Blackberry Smoke. Chris Stapleton. The new Brockton girls. Bandanas tied around their throats. Stomping in their heavy motorcycle boots, spilling wine from the big jug as they take long sloppy sips. Hooting laughter. Raucous and wild. Fearless. And so full of desire. Life. And they're still listening to Lynard Skynard. They're still listening to "Free Bird."

Shalanski at the Biker Bar

Redneck biker bar in Laconia—here to see Donnie's band Shalanski play a lot of Grateful Dead songs—but this is a scary place. Scruffy tough guys in trucker hats—and thick-necked bald guys in no hats—and one guy that looks and seems like a rabid badger—territorial, eyes flicking about looking for trouble. "Bad craziness," Hunter Thompson would have said. Fear and loathing in Laconia.

Donnie plays some reggae—and it doesn't go over so well— there's a tension in the place that feels like stale, polluted swamp gas. And Donnie keeps smiling. And then he moves on into some Grateful Dead—and a lot of tough, attractive looking tattooed women start to dance—and it's all o.k. They're fearless—and it's all about sex—and it all makes sense on some instinctual level—and the scruffy guys stay in their seats and at the bar, but they're moving to the music, plodding and nodding to Donnie's grooves—they start to look like professional wrestlers—the dirty but funny and interesting professional wrestlers with scraggily beards. They trust Donnie now, and it's all o.k.

Then Donnie's eyes phase out and drift into that faraway place—that place that he always goes to when he really gets into his music—and Donnie cuts loose in his guitar solo in the middle of "Sugaree"—the sound oozes out and subdues the crowd like a pleasant, dreamy narcotic cloud. Donnie touches a couple foot pedals next to the mic stand—and the world gets psychedelic—but smooth and easy—a mystical sensory pillow—and Donnie smiles—and scruffy people all over the bar smile—and nod—and soothe their souls. That's really why we all came here, I figure.

The Pants King

Zapanski was probably the weakest bowler on our team, but he was entertaining. His full name was Arnie Zapanski, but we just always called him Zapanski. He wore those round, metal-framed eyeglasses that turn of the century Russian revolutionaries wore. His head and hair always reminded me of a radish, for some reason.

The first time he bowled with us, someone on the other team though we were calling him "The Pants King," and they asked: "How did you get to be the Pants King?" So, that became his nickname. And he worked hard to live up to it. He started wearing these really big, puffy Russian Cossack-looking pants. Another time we were bowling and he was wearing very flowery pants that kind of looked like drapes—and someone on the other team called him "The Pants Queen." Zapanski seemed to like that name, too. But we stuck with "The Pants King," just to save him money on his wardrobe, and to make it easier for him to bowl. Those floor-length royal gowns can really mess up your approach when you're bowling.

Maggot Boy

Lincoln Meegan was in my class in third grade. He lived a few blocks down the street from us—in the dirtiest, most messed up house any of us had ever seen. The front door was always open—and there was no screen door—so flies and birds and squirrels could just drift on in—and there was all sorts of crap up on their roof—lawn chairs, socks, baby toys, underwear. And the lawn was never mowed— ever. Lincoln had a baby brother, maybe two years old, and one time he actually got lost in the high, high grass of their front yard.

Lincoln was a year younger than me—and his older brother Randy was a few years older. Randy was just nasty—to everyone—all the time—but he was especially nasty to Lincoln. The Meegans had one of those long strands of sticky tape hanging from their kitchen ceiling—to catch flies—and it was loaded—jam-packed with dozens of dead flies. One morning Randy took the fly-tape down and wrapped it around Lincoln's head—right before the school bus came. And Lincoln just left it on. Randy kept calling him "Maggot Boy." And the name caught on with other kids—first on our bus, and then even more at school, especially at recess.

Kids were teasing Lincoln when they called him Maggot Boy, but Lincoln actually seemed to like it, like it was a super hero name. And then it just wasn't any fun for us to tease him with it anymore. But it was still a good nickname. Maggot Boy. It had a nice ring to it.

Ship of Fools

Red-headed drunk guy in a Red Sox hat on the "Ship of Fools" live music harbor booze cruise gives his "girlfriend" his ATM card, and she tries it at the bank machine fifteen feet away. "Mike, it doesn't work," she calls. He smiles stupidly and shrugs, and she uses her card. She turns around with cash, and he asks her to get him a Sam Adams Summer Ale. She gives him the finger and goes upstairs to dance to "Sugar Magnolia."

Wal-Mart Trilogy (Wal-Mart in the Morning)

I. The Wal-Mart Couple

Wal-Mart—early on a weekday morning—scary as hell—especially in the grocery store part—people shopping who look like professional wrestlers—not the professional wrestlers you see on TV—but the ones who wrestle at local high schools for a hundred dollars a night—old and lopsided and creepy-looking. One guy—who looks like the largest lumberjack in the world—is actually barefoot—he has overalls on with one strap hanging down loose—his "woman" asks him something about fish sticks, and he says: "Rrrrrrr," kind of like a grizzly bear—and she seems to understand him.

She says something back to him—but more in something like dog barks than in human words—and then she laughs—a shrill, high-pitched witch's laugh—showing that she's missing a few teeth. I move quickly to the dog food aisle. Somehow I figure it'll be safer there.

II. The Joust

An incredibly old guy with a tiny, withered face—like a shrunken potato, and very thick eyeglasses—is driving around Wal-Mart in one of those mechanized yellow carts. The sound of the mechanized cart is very numbing. From the other direction, a very large woman who looks like a giant frog comes driving another yellow mechanized cart—and for a moment I think they might actually crash into each other. But then they both weave their mechanized carts, veering left, then right—and it looks like Shriners in the 4th of July parade.

The ancient potato-faced man sways his cart wide—almost out of control—and JUST misses the frog-like woman. But then he crashes into a display of artificial pork jerky—and it crashes down behind him. His mechanized yellow cart staggers to a stop—and he slowly looks back at the wreckage and says: "Hey, is that pork jerky? I was looking for that."

31

III. Check Out

I get in line at the Wal-Mart check-out behind an old guy with no apparent teeth and a flannel cap like the kind my mother made me wear in the winter—when I was three. The guy says something to me, but the only word I can make out is "mulch"—and then he laughs—a raspy, mad cackle—like something from the hillbillies in the movie "Deliverance." I figure that he probably has an ax in his car. I look around and notice that I'm the only person in the store not limping. I hit the exit as fast as I can. And I vow never to shop here stoned again.

Hazel and the Ear

One summer when I was about 20, I worked at a special ed camp called Shadybrook, and I had to work a lot with a girl named Hazel. Hazel was twelve years old, but she looked about 40—actually she kind of looked like Christopher Walken wearing a blond wig. She was partially deaf in one hear—and her other ear was just a fake plastic thing—it looked almost like a glob of Silly Putty. Hazel also had one enormous, bulging eye—that was always looking up at the sky, or the ceiling—even when she was sleeping. And Hazel couldn't really talk—she just sort of grunted—like she was starting to laugh—a belly laugh blurt.

Hazel had a good sense of humor—but she also had a wicked temper. One time I walked outside and saw Hazel sitting under a tree with Rick Travisano—the biggest stoner of all of the counselors at Shadybrook. Rick was just staring at Hazel's face for a while—and then he said to her: "Hazel, you are really, really fucked up"—and Hazel laughed her belly laugh and slapped Rick on the shoulder. She appreciated Rick—she liked hanging out with him more than anyone else.

But later on that day—when we were at the river—when I told Hazel that it was time to come back to camp—she got mad. She wanted to stay at the river. She stamped her feet and snorted—like a grizzly bear might snort. And then when I insisted—"No, really, Hazel, we have to go back to camp"—she stamped her feet again, in protest, and then she actually took off her fake ear and threw it at me. She hit me in the face with her ear—and then she sat down on the ground with her arms folded. And just for a minute I felt a little bit like Vincent Van Gogh's girlfriend. And then I sat down on the ground next to her. Eventually she looked at me, and I said: "You know, Hazel, Rick is right; you really are really, really fucked up." Then Hazel snorted out a laugh, and she slapped me on the shoulder. And then everything was O.K.

Zoo People

The summer Cal and I hitchhiked across the country together, we ended up in Missoula, Montana, each of us working a few days a week at an all-night bar / gambling place. So, we had a lot of time to just hang out and play, and we had a lot of very cheap Montana home-grown weed.

There was a tacky hotel on Pine Street—the street where we were living. The hotel had an indoor pool in it, and you could see the pool through three big picture windows, right from the sidewalk on Pine Street. It reminded Cal and me of zoos that had underwater exhibits for otters or seals—that you could watch through glass. So, sometimes when we had nothing better to do, we'd get high and bring lawn chairs down to those big picture windows, drink vodka tonics in Solo cups, and watch the humans in the tacky hotel swim, imagining that they were seals. We would point at them, and clap for them when they would dive into the pool.

Most of them just got annoyed with us, and they'd leave, or move over to the hot tub on the other side of the pool area, where we couldn't see them as well. But one very skinny older lady, probably in her late 70's, well, she really liked having us clap for her. She waved to us, and blew us kisses, and then she did some odd kind of water ballet dance for us. We were so impressed we gave her a very long standing ovation.

Time
(Babies With Futuristic Headphones)

The rock-band Pink Talking Fish burns into their booming cover version of "Time," and the crowd at the Flying Monkey Music Hall is throbbing to the music.

Just a few feet in front of me, I notice a young mother changing her baby's diaper on the floor—the baby, just a few months old, is wearing large, white, futuristic-looking head-phones, apparently to block out the loud music. It just seems so out of place—the baby, so clean and pure, so tiny and frail. It throws me off.

I turn away, behind me, and I see Kenny, the town drunk, the guy that's always sitting at the bar, in EVERY bar in town, every time I'm in any bar in town. Kenny—who ages faster than any human I've ever known—looking shrunken and withered, all life essence sapped out of his scrawny body, more like a cadaver than a living human. Kenny is nodding to the music, slowly. But Kenny throws me off, too. The picture doesn't fit the world of the music.

I turn back forward, and the young mother is now breast feeding her headphoned baby—smiling, swaying to the beat of the Pink Floyd song as she feeds her baby. And yes—it does fit—the world makes sense again in this moment, in this song. I get lost in the oozing guitar sound.

Later, between the final song and the encore, I come back to reality, and I become very much aware of the smell of poop, somewhere close to me—and I just can't tell if it's coming from the baby in front of me—or from Kenny behind me. I am really hoping it's the baby.

The Girl in the Springsteen Song

"Sandy, the fireworks are hailin' over Little Eden tonight / Forcin' a light into all those stoned out faces left stranded on this Fourth of July . . ."-----Bruce Springsteen, "4th of July Asbury Park (Sandy)"

Summer number seventeen. I remember riding shotgun in Wayne's Firebird convertible as we cruised down Route 84 to Wayne's brother's house on the New Jersey coast—arguing about what tape to play next. Wayne wanted to hear the Beach Boys—over and over. Summertime music. But once we hit the Jersey border, it had to be Springsteen.

Freedom summer. Wayne's brother and sister-in-law were both pretty cool, low-key types. They didn't care if we came in drunk at four in the morning, or if we came in at all. I got the feeling that they got stoned a lot, although they never did in front of us.

Walking down the boardwalk one night early on in the week with Wayne and his cousin Kenny who lived down there—the boardwalk was alive. We were buzzed and bopping, and we didn't have to sober up to go home. I was just being friendly with everyone I saw, calling out to everyone who looked cool. Cute girl sitting on a bench on the boardwalk answered me with the sweetest smile I'd seen all summer, so I spun around to talk to her—as Wayne and Kenny kept walking down the boardwalk laughing.

We sat on the bench together and talked. Her name was Sandy—she was sixteen and almost as drunk as I was. We talked for a long time. It was easy.

We hopped down to the beach and walked along the water. It was a beautiful night, clear and calm, with a gentle breeze. It didn't feel real. I put my arm around her. We drifted off away from the water and wound up sitting in the sand underneath the boardwalk, hugging and kissing—and I kept thinking about summertime songs—Springsteen songs.

"Oh love me tonight and I promise I'll love you forever . . ."

Sandy was tough. Straight dirty-blond hair, not quite reaching her shoulders. She dressed like a hippie mountain girl. Worn out, unbuttoned flannel shirt over a blue t-shirt, and faded jeans with Grateful Dead and Allman Brothers patches on them. She smiled at me and time stopped.

"You know," I said, "I think this has been just about the best night of my life."
She laughed—so hard that she doubled over. "You're full of shit," she said.
"No, I mean it. I mean, you . . . and the beach and everything . . ."
She held up her hand to stop me from talking. Then she kissed me.

I saw her a few more times that week—we just hung out on the boardwalk together. But then the night before Wayne and I had to head back home, I met Sandy behind the arcade. We got high with a few of her Dead Head friends— and then we headed back toward the arcade. It started to rain. Summer rain—soft and steady. We took refuge underneath the boardwalk. It was dripping water all around us, but we weren't getting wet. Sandy tugged at my shirt and looked at me with a big, sad smile.

"I'm really gonna miss you," she said. "Yeah."

"Love me tonight for I may never see you again / Hey Sandy girl . . ."

I remember asking Sandy for her address that night. She just looked at me, and said, "Why?"
"What do you mean, why? So I can write to you—that's why. I really like you."
"I like you too. It's been a great week. But you're going away now. Three hundred miles away."
"Yeah, but we can stay in touch . . ."
"Tell me something—how many girls' addresses or phone

numbers have you gotten and then just sort of forgotten after a while?"

"A few. Jesus. Why do you have to be so depressing?"

She laughed. "Sorry. Didn't mean to be. I had a great time with you. I'm glad I met you. Isn't that enough?"

I shrugged. I started to talk, but she put her finger on my lips. She smiled. And then she kissed me. And everything seemed all right.

"I remember, Sandy, girl /Na, na, na, na, na, baby."

Part II: "Electrified Skeletons"

Ronnie and the Stump

My Uncle Ronnie only had one arm. His left arm was just a stump, about eight inches long—it looked like a delicatessen baloney. He was a big guy—and a very funny guy. Silly funny. He would come up to you and put his arm around your shoulder—buddy-buddy like—only it wasn't an arm—it was an eight inch stump.

And when he got into a lively discussion with you, he'd gesture wildly with his stump and jab it into your face. He'd lost most of his left arm in "the big war"—I'm not sure how he really lost it—but whenever someone would ask him where he lost his arm, he'd say: "up some German's ass."

I was at my cousin's wedding—and my Uncle Dick was a little bit drunk—when he started talking about Ronnie. Evidently Ronnie had been a really wild and violent guy when he first got back from the war. Very bitter. He had a problem with authority. And back then he had a steel hook attached to the end of his stump. But he got into a lot of drunken bar brawls, and he did a lot of serious damage with the hook, so he had to take it off.

It was when he met my Aunt Angie that he got himself under control. She's even funnier than Ronnie—and tougher too. And Ronnie worshipped Angie—enough to stop cutting people in bars with his hook.

One time I was with Ronnie and Aunt Angie at the town carnival and a local cop was yelling at him for parking illegally. Ronnie got this steely glare in his eyes—and he called the cop a "dirty little maggot." After the cop saw Ronnie's stump, he let him stay parked where he was. Ronnie he winked at me—and then he asked the cop if he could help him find the rest of his arm. The cop said, "How would I do that," and Aunt Angie said, "By crawling up some German's ass." And then Ronnie patted the cop on the shoulder with his stump, and everything was O.K.

The Exploding Man

I.

In high school we all took turns driving to the "field parties" on Friday nights—no one really wanted to drive there because you had to drive through acres of corn stalks and broken beer bottles—in order to sit around a big bonfire and drink massive amounts of beer. Once when we were seventeen, Maynard's car got hit by another car while it was parked at a field party. Actually it was Maynard's father's car—and the rear fender got pretty mangled.

It was a little after one a.m. when we brought the car home—Mr. Maynard, an ex-marine, had been waiting up for us. He came out into the driveway. Maynard started to explain—but his father just put his hand up to shut him up. He crouched down to look at the fender—then he stood up, took a couple of steps toward Maynard, and then punched him as hard as he could—square in the chest. Maynard staggered back a couple of steps, but he didn't fall. He'd been expecting it.

II.

The summer we were twenty-one Maynard liked to go to this seedy stripper bar called the Rustic Café. One night I went with him, along with our friend Ronnie and this other guy named Lesarde. We had all known Lesarde in high school, and we had all thought that he was an asshole. But Lesarde just had a knack for inviting himself along with us places. He was a wiry, hyperactive guy with oily dark hair. And he never shut up.

Inside the Rustic Café, Maynard walked right to a table near the stage where the strippers danced—a table where a crusty old guy named Johnny was sitting. We had met Johnny at the Rustic the summer before. Johnny had a wooden leg, and he entertained the bar crowd by playing the spoons along with the juke box music as the strippers danced. The dancers all seemed to like Johnny—they let him pick out most of the songs.

Lesarde didn't like the Rustic—he said it was too much of a dive. He sat alone at a table near the door. Maynard called him over, but he just shook his head, stayed at his own table and sulked. Maynard said, "Fuck'im then," and he ordered a picher of Bud. Johnny had his wooden leg propped up on a chair, and he was wailing with his spoons to an old Allman Brothers song. When the song ended, the local toughs in the bar cheered and hooted—more for Johnny than the dancer. Maynard poured him a beer.

"Where ya' been, Johnny?" Maynard asked him. "Ain't seen you around for a while."
"I usually come in in the afternoons now. To get away from my wife."
"Afternoons?" Maynard said. "Don'cha work?"
"Nah. I'm retired now."
"What's that, Johnny?" Maynard bellowed out, "you're retarded?"
"Nooo," Johnny chuckled. "I'm retired."
"You don't look retarded, Johnny." Johnny howled and slapped Maynard on the back. Then he bought us shots of Jack Daniels.

Later on, wooden Johnny was trying to teach Maynard how to play the spoons, but Maynard couldn't get the hang of it— he kept dropping them.
"Forget it, Wild Man," Johnny said to him finally, "you're too stupit."
"Stupid?" Maynard snapped back. "You're the one who's retarded, Johnny."

"Nooo," Johnny laughed, slapping his wooden thigh.
An older man in a suit coat approached the stage waving a dollar bill—he tucked it into the dancer's garter belt, and she swooped down and kissed him. Moments later a penny clanked onto the stage floor. Then another penny hit the dancer on the chest.

42

"Hey, who the fuck's throwin' pennies?" she shouted out, looking in Lesarde's direction. No one said anything. "Well, just cut that shit out," she said. Then slowly she started dancing again.

A moment later, Lesarde stood up and threw a handful of change at the dancer as hard as he could, pelting her face and body.

"You filthy whore," he called out to her.

By the time we got over to Lesarde, Evie the biker barmaid was already pushing him toward the door.

"Fuck you, you pig," Lesarde hissed at her.

Marnard grabbed Lesarde by the sleeve of his plastic-looking leather jacket and tugged him out the door like an unruly dog, saying, "You stupid fucking asshole."

In the back seat of Maynard's car, Lesarde noticed that the sleeve of his leather jacket was torn, and he told Maynard that he was going to have to pay to have it fixed. Maynard just told him to "shut the fuck up," and then for a while Lesarde just sat in the backseat seething, breathing loudly through his nose. And then he started to mutter: first about the ripped jacket, then about the "fuckin' pig dancer," and then about the "fuckin' old loser with the wooden leg." Maynard told him to shut up again, and Lesarde sensed that Johnny was a touchy subject, so that's what he focused on. "Fuckin' drunken old bum, suckerin you guys into buyin' him drinks."

"We buy each other drinks," Maynard snapped at him. "He bought us shots—he's a good guy."

"He's a drunken fuckin' loser," Lesarde hissed back.
All of a sudden Lesarde lurched forward and grabbed Maynard around the throat, digging his fingernails deep into Maynard's Adam's apple. The car swerved wildly, but Maynard brought it to a skidding stop at the edge of someone's lawn.

Maynard exploded, spinning around gasping for breath, Lesarde's hands still latched onto his throat. He grabbed Lesard by the head and jerked him into the front seat— then he threw the door open and pulled Lesarde outside, heaving him into the middle of the lawn in a pile. I heard a few thumping punches—and in the darkness I could only make out their silhouettes—the primordial man holding his enemy's head in one hand, pounding it into the ground like a big stone—harder, and harder. Ronnie and I rushed over and pulled Maynard away. He spit on Lesarde.

"Asshole," he shouted. "Stupid fucking asshole—big deal about your piece of crap fake leather jacket—big deal! Here!" He tugged off his own denim jacket and violently tore off one of the sleeves and threw it at Lesarde. Then he just stood over Lesard, snorting like a wild beast. He kicked him in the stomach, and then he was done—I could tell by his eyes.
"Put him in the fucking car," he said to Ronnie. "Before I kill him."

We drove in silence to Lesarde's house. Ronnie helped him to his door. Maynard shuddered and shook his head, as if he had just taken a shower and his hair was wet. Then he pulled out of Lesarde's driveway.
"Why don't we go back to the Rustic," he said. "I want to buy Johnny and the dancer a few shots."

III.

Another summer visit home—and now twenty-five year old Maynard is an actual member of the local Elks club—just like his dad. Maynard's father is now retired—hanging out at the Elks club every weekend night. Maynard takes me and Ronnie there one Friday night—to drink and play pool. By 9:30 his father is already sloppy drunk, slurring words and telling endless war stories. Maynard screams at him to shut up. Mr. Maynard drunkenly slips off his barstool and crashes in a crumpled heap on the floor. Maynard brings his father out into the parking lot—and then he punches him—as hard as he can—square in the jaw. Mr. Maynard falls back against a car—but he doesn't fall. He'd been expecting it. We all had.

Meet Me at the Met

There used to be an old dive blues bar in Providence called the Met Café—a bunch of my writer friends would go there to drink Guinness stout and write group table poems. There was a very old Black man who was always there, dancing by himself, or sometimes he would conduct the band like an orchestra leader. His name was Frederick Watson Turner—supposedly he had once danced in a movie with Shirley Temple, a very long time ago. He used to just move up to someone in the bar and stare them in the eye for a long time. Sometimes he wouldn't say anything at all, just nod; but sometimes he would stare at someone for a long time and then say: "You're an asshole," in a low hiss, and then he'd dance away. As far as I could tell, he was always right. I used to buy him drinks, to stay on his good list; he liked bourbon on the rocks.

And there was usually a pretty rough-looking motorcycle gang at the Met, hanging out around the door, just acting mean. One night I came in wearing a red t-shirt with a picture of Leo Tolstoy on it, and one of the bikers stopped me. He thought it was a picture of "that I-ranian I-uh-tolah guy" on my shirt, and he said that he ought to kick the crap out of me just for being un-American. I told him that it wasn't the ayatollah, that it was Leo Tolstoy, the Russian novelist.

"Russian!" the biker screamed. "That's even worse. That makes you a Communist."

I tried to explain to him that Tolstoy had, in fact, written before the Bolshevik revolution, and that Russia hadn't become communist yet, but he didn't seem interested in that. He grabbed me by the shirt collar and twisted it in his fist.

That's when Frederick came over. Frederick Watson Turner--sort of slid in between the biker and me, moving to the music of the blues band, shaking his head and waggling his finger at the biker. The biker broke his hold on me. Frederick pointed his bony finger at the biker's face and hissed: "asshole." The biker looked down at the floor, deflated, like a guilty child, like the Wicked Witch of the West at the end The Wizard of Oz. And then, Frederick patted the biker on the shoulder, and everything was O.K. again. Frederick moved back off to dance in front of the stage again, and I moved off to buy him a bourbon on the rocks.

I had to pay my dues.

Animal

My old roommate, Donnie, used to keep an old wooden chair leg under the driver's seat of his car—it was thick, heavy wood, more like the leg of a sturdy coffee table. He said it was "for emergencies."

I didn't really know Donnie all that well—he'd only been my roommate for one semester my first year at college—and even then he wasn't around a lot. He'd grown up in town, and he stayed at his father's house down by the beach in Narragansett every weekend. And after Christmas he moved back home for good.

I'd come back to Rhode Island that summer weekend to stay with Donnie, hang out at the beach, and drink a lot of beer. We did that. And when Donnie drank—even just a couple beers—he got belligerent. A vicious wild animal.

Donnie was driving late Friday night—fast and reckless—weaving in and out of beach town traffic—and another car—a black Firebird—cut him off at an intersection, very narrowly missing his car. Donnie caught up with the Firebird at the next traffic light—he laid on his horn and gave the driver the finger. The driver of the Firebird—another rowdy 20 year-old—gave him the finger right back.

"You fucking ass-hole!" Donnie screamed at him. The other driver leaned out of the Firebird and spit—a thick mack at Donnie's windshield. That was it. In a split second, Donnie grabbed his chair leg, hopped out of the car, and completely smashed in the rear windshield of the Firebird in an explosion of broken glass.

A police cruiser was waiting on the opposite side of the traffic light. It flew over to us, flashers on. Donnie, still holding his chair leg in his hand, screamed out at the cop: "Officer, arrest this man—he spit on my car."

Later on, after Donnie's father bailed him out of jail, Donnie stopped at the counter at the front of the police station and asked the arresting officer if he could have his chair leg back. "Uh, could I have my little toy back," he said, somehow reminding me of Tony Montana in Scarface—with his blind arrogance. The cop stared at him, incredulous. "Get the hell out of here," he said.

My old roommate Donnie used to keep an old chair leg under the driver's seat of his car. He said it was "for emergencies." I guess, for Donnie, an "emergency" was any time another wild animal looked him directly in the eye. Or maybe just when someone left the door of his cage open.

Snake Charmer

Ben's house—on a muddy brown pond in southern Rhode Island—Ben and Steve are stoned—and Ben takes off his shirt and stomps into the pond in just his jeans, screaming out that he's going to catch a fish—"just like a bear"—with his bare hands. He splashes around a while, grabbing into the water like a primordial beast—"He is like a bear," Steve says. Ben gets frustrated and dives under the water—he's under for a while. When he comes back up—with another primordial shriek—he's holding a black snake in his fist.
"I hypnotized it with my left hand," he says, showing us—pulsing his fingers open-closed, open-closed—"and then I caught it with my right hand."

"What're you going to do with it?" Steve asks.
"I don't know," Ben answers. "Wanta eat it?"
"No," Steve says, in his mellow monotone. "No thanks, I'm good . . . besides, snakes are evil."
Ben laughs. "Then we'll give it a joy ride," he says. "Snakes must wanta know how it feels to fly—we all do." And he spins around in circles a few times, holding the snake out at arm's length—and then he lets it go—and it flies—in a high, graceful arc, and then it disappears into the water with a soft plunk.

"Wow," Steve says to me. "That's the most beautiful thing I've ever seen happen to a snake."

Transformer Man

My friend Steve used to look at people and see them with animal faces--usually apes-- but sometimes pigs or dogs or bugs of some sort. I thought that was odd at first--that maybe it had something to do with Steve being stoned so much of the time. But now, I just don't know.

One time I was having lunch with Steve at the El Phoenix on Comm. Ave., and I asked him about his animal visions. He gestured to the waiter, a stumpy guy who had a thick, dark uni-brow and a sharply protruding ape-like jaw. "Look," Steve said, "he's still in the process of transforming." The waiter grunted at us and hopped away clumsily.
  I could sort of see what he meant. He was an ape.

"And look over there--look at that guy," Steve said, pointing. There was a "man" at the table to our right, eating some sort of casserole plate—or perhaps it was shepherd's pie. Anyway, the man had his face lowered over the plate and he was hoovering up mashed potatoes and corn and ground beef ravenously—without efficiently using utensils. When he finally raised his face from the plate, it was covered with potatoes and brown gravy.

"I know he's got a lot of slop on his face," Steve said, but if you look closely just above the guy's mouth you can detect the beginnings of a large pig-snout. Oh, he's a pig all right."

As if on cue the pig man snorted, and then mashed his face back into his casserole plate. Steve shook his head. "He ought to eat out of a trough," he said.

"Yeah, I sort of see it," I said. "So, is it usually apes and pigs that you see people turn into?"

"Well, yeah, a lot of apes," Steve said, "but it's more varied than that." He looked around the restaurant for an example. Off in a dark corner, a couple in their early 20's sat, very seriously kissing each other. Both wore dark, polyester
50

clothing and a lot of jewelry, and both had very dark hair that appeared to be wet. Their kissing became more involved—more intense—their wet faces became plastered to each other—two large, oozing slugs sealing into each other. "There, over there, see them, that 'couple' over there---what do they look like to you?"

"Slugs?" I said.

"Yes," he said. "Exactly. They make me sick."

Later on we were walking across the common, and it started to hit me. Steve was on to something. He was just more observant than most people.

A teen-aged couple playfully pranced by us. They were down on all fours on the grass, hopping about each other like excited dogs—taking turns sniffing each others' butts.

"Dog people," I said, pointing. Steve nodded.

"Some days I worry that I might forget what it's like to be human," he said, watching the puppy couple. And then he sighed. "But even so," he went on, "it's still way better than when I see people turning into machines." He stopped and shook his head.

Wow, I thought, Steve sees machine heads. That's when I started worry.

Border Patrol

Hitchhiking somewhere on I-90 in eastern Minnesota Cal and I got picked up by a couple of good ole boys in a jeep, with a cooler full of beer. Heileman's Special Export. They were driving all the way to South Dakota just to buy fireworks. Getting drunk along the way. The driver had on an old baseball cap that said: "Fuck Iran." And he was really proud of it.

And so we drank a lot of Heileman's Special Export beer, and every once in a while one of the guys up front would just go—Yeeeeeeeeeee—haah! And every once in a while, the driver, Paul, would yell out—PISS—CALL! And he'd pull over to the breakdown lane, get out of the jeep, climb up on the hood, and piss—long distance . . . usually calling out some fitting expression, like—"Niagara Falls! . . . Yeeeeeeeeeeee—haah!"

And so it was early evening by the time the Minnesota rednecks dumped us off, drunk out of our minds, on the side of route 90, just over the South Dakota border. They headed off in their Fuck-Iran hats to buy the South Dakota fireworks that they had so coveted. And there we were, stuck on the roadside, too wasted to budge our duffel bags, too wasted to even bother sticking out our thumbs. Too wasted to do anything but fight with each other. Drunk—and after six days living on the road together, we were definitely in the mood to fight. And I knew just the right thing to say to make Cal really mad. I called him a phony intellectual snob. And from there it didn't take us long to just start shouting "fuck you" at each other at the tops of our lungs.

And that's when a big old Plymouth Fury pulled over, right in front of us. And we hadn't had our thumbs out or anything. The car just pulled over, then backed up and stopped right beside us. A drunken middle aged woman rolled down the window and asked us if we-all were wantin' a ride. Her hair looked like it was covered in black shoe polish. The same look as her caked-on eye make-up, that looked like she'd put it on with a trowel. We didn't say anything. We just threw our duffel bags into the back seat and climbed in beside them. They were drinking some kind of clear, strong-smelling alcohol out of peanut butter jars. They asked us questions, but we ignored them for the most part. We were still too busy fighting.

They asked us if we wanted a drink, and the one riding shot-gun dangled her bare foot over the car seat, trying to be sexy, I guess. But Cal just looked at the foot and started to laugh. It was a pretty funny sight. It was a long, hairy foot with deep red nail polish. And once Cal started laughing, I couldn't help but laugh too. And then we couldn't stop. And the ladies, well they got real pissed. They pulled the car over and called us "Yankee faggots" and told us to get the fuck outa their car.

So, we hopped out, and just sorta fell on the ground laugh-ing out of control. And we laughed and rolled around for a long time. Until we felt it start to rain. The rain felt good, refreshing. For about twenty minutes. And then it got an-noying. And it started to rain harder. We walked a half mile or so, to a highway rest area with cement picnic tables with individual roofs over them. Cal and I each claimed a table, and lay down on it, and passed out.

I woke up with an aching back and a piercing hangover headache. But then I looked up, and saw the sun just start-ing to break over the mountains---and it just took the wind out of me--it was so fucking beautiful. I had to wake Cal. And we stared at the rising sun in dumb reverence for a good half-hour, awestruck. It was so amazing that we forgot that we hated each other's guts. And we figured out why we were hitchhiking across the country in the first place.

"Flies"

The summer we lived in Missoula, Montana, Cal and I smoked a lot of pot. We both had jobs at bars, working a few nights a week—and we had a really cheap place to live— so we bought a shoebox full of Montana homegrown and smoked three or four joints a day.

Cal started saving our roaches—and half-smoked joint-buts—first in a coffee cup—but then in a white business-size envelope; he printed the word "roaches" on it—and left it on our coffee table.

We always had a lot of flies in our apartment that summer, so I got a wooden ruler and a big rubber band, and I started hunting flies. I had a lot of free time on my hands that summer—so I did a lot of fly hunting. Seeing Cal's "roach" envelope, I decided to start a collection of my own. I got another white business envelope and printed the word "flies" on it. By the end of the summer, when we were leaving Montana, there must have been 60 or 70 flies in the envelope.

On the day we had to move out of our apartment, I just couldn't bring myself to throw the flies away—and I thought of my friend Steve back in Providence. Steve was the lead singer in a punk rock band called Living with the Bomb, and he was a little twisted, so I thought that he'd appreciate the flies. I took the envelope full of flies—as it was—and sealed it, and on the front of the envelope where it was labeled, I wrote: "flies" c/o Steve Sutton, 15 Wiggins St., Providence, RI 02909. I put an extra stamp on it, and I mailed it.

Two weeks later, while I was still on the road, a 6"x9"manila envelope arrived through the mail at my parents' house in Connecticut. On the front of the envelope it read: "Dead Snake" c/o Matt Lucas, 15 Warren Ave., Rockville, CT.

That's the last time my mother ever opened up my mail.

The Pigeon Wars

Day I.

The Central Connecticut Co-Op Feed Mill factory--in Manchester, CT--the worst job I've ever had. Mind numbing work--amidst mind-numbing machines--loading animal feed into trucks, shoveling corn and chemicals, cleaning storage bins and silos. Machine head syndrome. My co- workers--sideshow freaks--they limp about with molasses-like ooze running down from their nostrils, like Hitler moustaches from breathing in the bonding chemicals that fill the air here. They laugh at me because I'm the only one here who wears the surgical masks they make available to save our lungs. The walking dead.

I get stoned with Donnie, one of the younger truck drivers, during the morning coffee break. And then, since there's no boxcar to unload, I am sent to Warehouse #4 to clean chemical dust, because the dust and grain keeps jamming the conveyer belt gears there.

Warehouse #4--a cold, tin hut--home to a vicious gang of evil pigeons. Mean pigeons--they line up and glare at me from the top of the machine. It's their building. Their eyes follow me everywhere, as I try to clean--but they're freaking me out. I get out of there as fast as I can.

Day II.

It's back to Warehouse #4 again, first thing in the morning--but this time I'm psychologically prepared for the psycho-pigeons. They're there, waiting for me, the evil horde--glaring at me--leering. On an impulse, I pick up a piece of heavy copper pipe and hurl it--with all my might--at the middle of the pigeon row--dead on--I hit one. The others scatter in chaos. Small victory.

Day III.

There seem to be more pigeons than usual in Warehouse #4 today. A lot more. And they're bigger--with seemingly more human characteristics. There is a definite leader among the pigeons--a massive bird--that looks like Anthony Hopkins in his Hannibal Lectur movies. Another pigeon clearly looks just like Christopher Walken.

They all watch me--intensely--they shriek at me. Their shrieks are taunts--beyond warnings--they're not telling me to get out--they're telling me it's too late--that I've already gone too far. I am a condemned man. They're a ruthless, bloodthirsty gang.

They swoop--dive-bombing me--closer and closer to my head. I cower in a corner-- occasionally swatting at them feebly with my broom. When there's an opening, I make a run for it--slamming the warehouse door behind me--and I run for safety in the bathroom in the mill--until I stop shudder-ing. The pigeons have won.

Day IV.

Ashamed of myself for my cowardice--the next morning, I wake up mean. I look in the mirror feeling like Pink in the movie Pink Floyd: The Wall. No shaving, no washing, no breakfast. No rational thought. I look around for a weapon, and I find part of a Halloween costume I wore a few years ago--a giant chicken head. I have to sneak it in to work in a black plastic garbage bag.

Warehouse #4. Yes, the row of biker pigeons is as big and fierce as ever. Anthony Hopkins is prominent, front and cen-ter. Watching me. I turn away from them briefly, like an impressionist getting into character--and I pull on the giant chicken head. With a fearsome burst of energy--all that I have--I spin around and run directly at the pigeons. Many scatter--but Anthony Hopkins stays put, ten feet above me--watching.

56

I dance, stomping about in front of him--I had intended it to be an aboriginal war dance --but I don't know how to do any aboriginal war dances--so it ends up more like a mosh-pit slam dance--Ramones music fills my head--Beat on the brat with a baseball bat!--Hey-ho--the Blitzkrieg bop—Labotomy! Labotomeee! I lose myself in the dance.

The next thing I know, Donnie is in the warehouse--the boss has sent him to get me to come down for lunch. Donnie is sitting down in the corner by the door--laughing so hard that he is convulsing. But I look up at the pigeons. They are calm. Anthony Hopkins bows to me in respect.

I go down to the main office and give the boss my two weeks notice. There's just no reason to come back.

Pain Aids

I was playing on the Penwood State Park employee softball team with an odd mix of young neo-hippies, crusty farmer types, and a few 20 year-old city punks who were part of some federal employment program. Our official team name was the "Penwood State Park Pileated Woodpeckers," but our uniform T-shirts just said: "Penwood Peckers."

And everyone on the team was number 69.

Just prior to our "big game" against our rival, People's State Forest, our hippie centerfielder Ted brought out a carton of something labeled "Pain Aids." Ted's uncle was a foreman at a textile mill, where they freely distributed Pain Aids to their workers—to get the most work possible out of them. Pain Aids were primarily a mixture of aspirin and caffeine, plus some kind of muscle stimulant, in pill form. Ted gave each player on our team a handful of Pain Aids, claiming that they would make us "wicked fast," and also that we wouldn't get a headache for weeks. So most of us took twelve or more—even though the carton said that the maximum dosage was four.

But the Pain Aids didn't make us fast at all. We all just stood around feeling wooden and cranky and strung out. A ball would go by us in the field and we'd just stare at it angrily and refuse to move. I was playing third base, and someone hit a looping popup to me in the first inning, and as I watched it descend it turned into a series of overlapping squares, kind of like a cubist painting by Picasso. It looked like a box kite, but with sharp teeth. I dove out of the way and let it plop to the ground. And the players on the People's State Forest team also started to look very scary to me--like electrified scare-crows with angry faces. They beat us real bad.

So we lost the game by 15 runs, and we were cranky and numb, and none of us could get to sleep at all that night. But none of us got hurt. And we all decided that Pain Aids and softball didn't mix. And so then our second baseman Phil said that he was going to bring a bag of hallucinogenic mush-rooms to the next game. We figured it was worth a try.

58

Giant Rat

There was a giant rat that lived in our basement floor apartment in Boston that year. I lived with two guys that I didn't know very well—and we were all very different personality types. One guy, Tom, worshipped David Bowie. He was a skinny, angular blond guy—with David Bowie hair and clothes. He called himself "Major Tom." The other guy was Irish Mike. Irish Mike liked the Pogues and the Dropkick Murphies, and all things Irish.

The three of us didn't have a lot of common interests to talk about. Therefore, we got stoned a lot, and we'd sit around in the living room—which was also where Irish Mike slept—and zone out, watching TV. And the giant rat would lumber across the living room floor, waddling like an armadillo. And we'd be dazed and numbed out, but we appreciated having the rat to focus on. "Holy crap," someone would say, "that rat is huge!" "It's more like a dog."

The rat would squeeze into a hole behind the radiator in Irish Mike's room and disappear. But then one day the giant rat got stuck. We could hear it—wedged in between the wall and a stud or a pipe in the corner of the living room. It would emit a low squeak and wiggle and push.

We told our landlord about it, but he just sent over an exterminator who left a lot of trays full of poison lying around the apartment. That was the end of the giant rat.

It was sad, like losing a pet. And we didn't talk to each other about it. We just went about our lives, sharing the painful, tragic glances of parents who silently mourn their lost children.

The GoodTime Bar

The GoodTime Bar—in downtown Lafayette, Indiana—
"where every night is Halloween." Stiff Kitten, a heavy
metal hair-band cranks out Ratt and Motley Crue covers—to
sweaty bikers and local metal-heads—cramped together into
this seedy shack. Wiry biker chick in a fight with her boy-
friend—lifts him up by his t-shirt and rams the back of his
head against the battered wall—making the tables in the back
shake—and the skinny, middle-aged drying out ex-drunk
bartender looks nervous—too scared to pick up the baseball
bat behind the bar. So then the heavy metal hair-band breaks
into AC/DC—just to help break up the brawl—just to make
everyone happy.

Hunter Thompson's Ashes

"Our vibrations were getting nasty . . . Had we deteriorated
to the level of dumb beasts?"
-----Raoul Duke, from
Fear and Loathing in Las Vegas

Fear and loathing in Boulder, Colorado.

I was visiting my friend Jack in Boulder, and we went
to this party in a big house up on a cliff. There were two
skinny guys in their mid-twenties, both wearing aviator
sunglasses, snorting lines of something gray at the kitchen
table. A middle-aged bald guy was setting them up, but not
snorting himself. Jack asked them if they were doing coke,
and one of them smiled and said: "No way, man. This is way
better than coke. This is the ultimate trip."

The bald guy told us that they were snorting the ashes of
Hunter S. Thompson, the famous writer and gonzo journalist. This guy, who introduced himself as Gerard, told us
that he worked at a crematorium in Aspen—and that he had
personally done the Hunter Thompson cremation. The two
skinny guys in sunglasses were now smoking cigarettes in
cigarette holders, just like Hunter Thompson's. They both
started to mutter about seeing bats in the room, sounding
just like Johnny Depp in Fear and Loathing in Las Vegas.

"Oh, that's bullshit," Jack said to the bald guy. "They shot
Hunter Thompson's ashes into space with a cannon—Johnny
Depp did it."

"No," Gerard said. "Those weren't his real ashes. I just
gave them a tin full of regular old ashes—mostly from my
barbecue."

Gerard then tried to sell us a vile of Thompson's ashes--
$300 for a bottle about the size of his pinky. He said it was
enough for both of us—enough for "four good-sized lines."

"Gerard, why the fuck would we want to snort Hunter
Thompson's ashes?" Jack said.

Gerard smiled. "For three or four hours you'll get to feel like Hunter S. Thompson. You'll see his visions. You'll experience what it was like to be Doctor Gonzo."

"So it would be kind of like reading one of his books?" I said.

Jack was pissed. "This is just such bullshit," he said. "It's just burnt up skin and bone and tissue. It's not a fucking brain transplant." Jack walked out of the room, shaking his head.

Later on, Jack came out of the bathroom holding a plastic Solo cup full of urine. He brought the cup to the kitchen table and put it down in front of the two skinny guys in sunglasses. "Here," he said. "This is Jack Nicholson's piss. If you drink it, you'll be wicked cool."

One of the skinny guys looked up and stopped trying to act like Hunter Thompson for a minute. "No way," he said. "For real?" He tilted his head and looked at his friend. They were actually considering it.

Johnny Fist

A muscle-bound young blond man strode up to the bar and slapped both of his palms down hard on the wooden counter to get Sherry's attention. She looked at him, expressionless. He held up six fingers.

"Six beers for Johnny Fist." He was wearing a tight t-shirt that read: "Johnny Fist will Kick some Ass tonight."

"The limit is two," Sherry answered flatly, putting down two bottles.

Johnny Fist threw some bills onto the bar and smiled, picking up the beers.

"I'll be back," he announced.

I'd only been working at the bar for a couple weeks. I'd never seen this guy before. "What's the deal with the inflatable man?" I asked Sherry.

"Johnny Fist? He's here quite a bit. He's a small time professional wrestler—you know, like in that movie with Mickey Rourke. He wrestles down at the armory—I guess he almost always loses. Somebody told me his tights have a black circle on the crotch, with a bright red fist in the center."

"Figures," I said, watching Johnny as he worked his way over to a table of girl-women near the bar.

"Who's got a cigarette for Johnny Fist?" he barked out.
A girl in leather jacket gave him one. Johnny Fist nodded.

"Johnny Fist likes action," he said with a smile.

"Oh Jesus," I said, shaking my head.

"He's all talk," Sherry said. We watched him pose for the girl-women, flexing his muscle. "I carded him the first time he came in." Sherry smiled. "His real name is Wendell."
She shook her head. "And Wendell is a really shitty tipper."

Addicts

I was in my early twenty's, working lunches as a waiter at Giorgio's Italian Restaurant just outside of Boston—and I got asked out on a date by a 40 year old recovering cocaine addict with three kids who was on parole for punching another woman. She wanted me to go to a karaoke bar with her. Her youngest son used to come in to get Cokes to go, and he always had to flatten his dollar bills out before he would give them to me—so that they didn't have any wrinkles in them. His mother said that growing up in a crack house will do that to a person.

Lesarde

In high school, Lesarde had done some pretty weird things. Mainly to get attention. Once he shaved his head completely bald to win a five dollar bet--and he never got paid. Another time he ran around the cafeteria naked--chasing people with an ice cream scoop.

He first name was Laird, but everyone just called him "Lesarde," his last name. He really hated his first name. Every once in a while--like in the middle of a class when we were taking a test--out of nowhere he would just scream out: "I can't believe my parents fucking named me Laird!"

Lesarde had a brother a year younger than him--and HE was actually the troubled one in the family. His name was Eulin, but everyone called him "Urine." He had a job cooking at the local Friendly's, but he got fired for doing obscene things to the food.

Even though Laird Lesared was in the same grade as me, he was older than most of my friends, and he had his own car by sophomore year in high school, so people hung out with him--mainly just to get rides. One time he was driving me home from school and he had to stop at his house to pick something up, so I went into his house for just a minute. There were a lot of paintings of naked men on the walls. And in the middle of the living room there was a giant birdcage, the size of a telephone booth--with the door open. Lesarde told me that his father liked to sit inside the cage for hours at a time with the door shut. I just wanted to get the fuck out of there.

I saw Lesarde a few years after graduation--he was working at Burger King. He pretty much looked the same as he had in high school, but on one side of his head his hair was dyed black and the other was bleached blond. And his name tag said: "Larry." I asked him about the name tag. He put his finger to his lips and whispered: "I'm just going by Larry now." And then he got a faraway look in his eyes. His face contorted in anger, and then through clenched teeth he said: "I can't believe my parents fucking named me Laird." But then he calmed right back down again and added: "Oh, do you want fries with that?"

The Subterraneans

It seemed like at least half of my friends at college were stoner-hippie-Dead Heads--but I also had a lot of punk rocker friends--I just didn't party much with them at night--so I didn't really see them in their punk element. But then one time Iggy and Steve--our closest friends that were serious punks--invited us to a big party at their house.

I went to the party with my hippie roommates Jack and Cubby--and early on in the evening everything was fine. It seemed like a regular party. It wasn't that crowded yet-- and they were playing music that we were pretty familiar with-- the Talking Heads, Elvis Costello--we felt safe with it. Yeah, we were the only people there not dressed entirely in black, but we were having fun--mingling with punks.

But then something happened. It seemed to get a lot more crowded--with scarier looking punks. And then most of the lights went out, and somebody put on a Ramones album--and cranked it. And all of a sudden it was like the punks became possessed.

They went nuts--lurching and jumping and moshing--slam dancing--smashing violently into each other--into us--all to blaring Ramones machine-gun music: "Lobotomy! Lobotomy!" The walls started to close in on me. And by the time they put on the Sex Pistols album, I was stumbling around frantically looking for Jack and Cubby. I needed air.

Outside, I found Cubby sitting on a rock next to the field behind the house, freaking out. He was shaking. "I can't go back in there, Matty," he said. "There's evil in there."

Eventually Steve came out looking for us. He helped settle Cubby down--with some very soothing Lebanese hash. And then he got Cubby to go back inside the house--partly by promising him that he'd play some Neil Young music.

And by the end of the night, Cubby had gotten most of the punks involved in burning a zorch with him. Cubby loved making zorches. He'd twist a couple of plastic garbage bags together, tie knots in them, and then hang them from the ceiling and set the bottom of it on fire--and have the burning, melting plastic stutter-drip down into a bucket of water. It looked like a special effect from Star Wars. The punks watched the zorch, fascinated, completely zoned out--staring in amazement as the melted plastic formed a little floating, burning island of melted glop in the bucket.

Steve put on a Patti Smith album and asked us to "give it a chance." "Hey, it's a lot better than disco," he said. And he was right. The melted plastic island got us thinking about how much we all hated disco. We had a common bond. And Patti Smith sounded pretty good--doing her beat-like poetry rants. And everything was O.K. after that. The party got a lot better.

Part III:
"Meat Sculptures"

Looking for Jack Kerouac's Grave

Driving up I95 north in Steve's Oldsmobile, heading for Jack Kerouac's grave in Lowell, Mass. It was all Ben's idea. It was the anniversary of Kerouac's death, October 21st, and Ben was pretty sure we'd see Bob Dylan up at Kerouac's grave. Ben and me in the back sharing a gallon of red Gallo wine, Scarlette is up front with Steve, riding shotgun, rolling a joint—in her overdyed black hair and heavy black eye make-up. Scarlette is the bass player in Steve's punk rock band "Living With the Bomb," and like Steve she is dressed all in black, and like Steve, she doesn't smile or talk very much. They are drinking generic beer out of white cans with only the word "beer" printed on them in black—like the cans labeled "food" in "Repo Man." Steve takes a small brown bottle out of his suit jacket pocket, twists off the cap and takes a deep sniff. Then he hands it to me. "Amyl nitrate," he tells me. "Also know as 'Locker Room.'" He puts Social Distortion on the tape player and cranks it, and Rhode Island turns into a psychedelic blur.

Somewhere north of Boston Steve stops at a grocery store, saying he wants to get some bread. We wander in and stray off in different directions. Ben climbs into the frozen food bin and lies down on top of the fish sticks and tater tots, folding his hands over his chest like a corpse. A woman sees him and screams. I find an intercom for the supermarket's public address system, and I start making grocery-related announcements taken from an Allen Ginsberg poem: "Walt Whitman to the meat counter please . . . Garcia Lorca to the melon section." Somewhere on the other side of the store I hear Scarlette laughing.

Out in the parking lot, Steve takes four loaves of Italian bread out of his grocery bag, giving each of us a loaf to bludgeon each other with, "Kind of like a pillow fight," he tells us. In a matter of minutes all of our loaves are smashed to smithereens. Steve pulls one final loaf out of his bag and hands it to me. "Here," he says, "hold this with both hands while I do smite it with mighty blows."

The police arrive just as we are exiting the parking lot, resuming our search for Jack Kerouac's grave. Somehow we get lost, and wind up stumbling around what we believe is a cemetery. In reality it's just some sort of public memorial to local war heroes. Regardless, Steve is convinced that he has found Jim Morrison's grave, and that it spoke to him. So he's happy.

The trip ends at a bar in Boston called The Rat, where Someone and the Somebodies are playing garage-punk, and Scarlette has gotten us all in for free. Ben starts to complain about our never having found Jack Kerouac's grave. "We weren't supposed to," Scarlette tells him in her husky monotone. "Graves are for dead people. We just needed a reason to move." Ben bellows out his crazed, primordial laugh, and then he starts to dance wildly, out of control in his beat-up hiking boots. We all do.

My Friend Steve

My friend Steve used to work in the deli at Stop n' Shop, cutting and weighing meat. He wore a little plastic nametag that read: "Dr. Sahib." Dr. Sahib was the name of Steve's punk rock band, and it was also the name of one of Steve's heroes. Dr. Sahib was a vigilante who lived in China and went around to the prison cells of convicted rapists and murderers very late at night and poked their eyes out with a bicycle spoke.

My friend Steve used to work in the deli at Stop n' Shop. Steve was an art major, and he used to make sculptures out of meat which he would bring home from work. The meat sculptures would turn various colors as they began to decay. Steve referred to them as "kinetic art." The curator of the student art gallery would not allow Steve's meat sculptures to be kept inside the gallery with the other works of art—so they would be left outside of the art building where they would be eaten by dogs and other local animals.

My friend Steve used to work in the deli at Stop n' Shop, and he used to get stoned several times a day. He loved to operate the electric meat slicer, but he would sometimes phase out and slice off the tip of one of his fingers, bleeding profusely on the Stop n' Shop meat. Every week when I'd shop there, Steve would wave from behind the counter, sporting a new heavily bandaged finger.

My friend Steve used to work in the deli at Stop n' Shop, but he got fired. His boss said that he was making the customers sick, what with the severed fingers and all. But that was years ago. Now Steve works a the Encyclopedia Britanica in Chicago. He's a chief indexer. He doesn't make sculptures anymore—perhaps because he lost his ready supply of Stop n' Shop meat. Now he has his own office and makes a lot of money. And he hasn't seriously cut himself in years. My friend Steve used to work in the deli at Stop n' Shop—but I guess we all have to grow up sometime.
'

Angel of the Dog Track

It'd been my idea to go to the dog track, to see the grey-hounds race. I wanted to find Charles Bukowski, or Ernest Hemingway's grandson, or at least some worldly wise, romantically battered street-poets living on the razor's edge. My friend Missaiko went along, to drink and to win some money. And Jeff just went along. Just to see what it was like, I guess.

Anyway, the whole scene couldn't have been more sad. Constipated dogs shaking, emaciated, futilely attempting to crap on the track. Wilted, pathetic men completely devoid of energy. Devoid of life. Two or three of them in wheel-chairs. Faded rejects from a Bruce Springsteen Nam Vet video. Missaiko really looked out of place: tan, muscular, fiery. He weaved his way through the withered losers, shout-ing at them contemptuously: "Yeah, yeah, what's your sad story, Loser." He went up to a strung-out looking guy on the floor, wearing cracked, plastic-looking shoes with a hole in the sole. "Yeah, there goes the rent, you fucking sad sack," Missaiko shouted at him.

Jeff just drifted around, chatting easily with strangers, looking angelic in his crumpled white shirt, blonde curls, and childlike smile.

I kept betting two-dollar quinellas and losing. Missaiko won forty dollars early on and ended up coming out about even. Jeff didn't bet. On the last race of the night, I talked him into making one bet. He bet the number three dog to win—his favorite number. The three dog was twelve-to- one. It won. Jeff smiled and shrugged, and gave his winning ticket to the guy on the floor with the plastic shoes, and he just said, "Here, I found this, I think it must be yours."

The guy on the floor stared at Jeff, his jaw quivering, as if he were looking at a ghost—as if, all of a sudden, he could believe in God again.

Feeding Aunt Lottie

Bringing Thanksgiving dinner to my Aunt Lottie was one of those holiday duties that no one ever wanted to get stuck with. Aunt Lottie was a wheelchair-ridden invalid, who shouted all the time and never chewed her food. She lived alone in one of the apartments in the senior citizen complex in the old part of town.

The Thanksgiving when I was 15, my mother decided that all three of us kids should bring Aunt Lottie her dinner together. Since my sister had just gotten married earlier that year, my mother saw this as an opportunity for her to re-bond with my brother and me. So, we went as a team.

Aunt Lottie sat in her wheelchair, watching us with her saggy eyes and her droopy, Saint Bernard jowls. She looked like "Mama" from the Danny Devito movie Throw Mama From the Train. She couldn't hear very well, so she shouted every time she spoke. "You wanta beer or suntin'!" she yelled to me. Being 15, I was thrilled and delighted to be offered a beer from anyone. I opened the refrigerator and pulled out an old bottle of Schlitz. "Schlitz!" said my brother Mark, who was 21, "I didn't know they still made that stuff." The bottle cap came off without my even twisting it, and my hand became covered in a brown molasses-like goo. I looked at the gooey beer bottle and thought of a story by Steven King where a man drinks a bacteria-filled beer and turns into a giant, scummy gray fungus. But I was 15, so I drank the beer anyway, even though it smelled like a sewer.

In the meantime Aunt Lottie had begun savagely hoovering down the Thanksgiving dinner we'd brought—like a wild dog, her head flopping as she grunted away. All of a sudden Aunt Lottie started to choke on a piece of turkey— big-eyed, gasping for breath, waving her chubby hands around. "What do we do?" Mark asked. "Slap her on the back," I said. "No," my sister said, "She's got really bad rheumatoid arthritis—she'll bruise." We all looked at each other and shrugged, and then my sister commenced to wailing on Aunt Lottie's back with her open palm. My brother Mark started to tell Aunt Lottie a story about a friend of his who'd recently found a mouse mixed in with his Kentucky Fried Chicken. I went to the emergency call switch, located in every room of the senior apartments, and I was just about to pull the string when the turkey became dislodged from Aunt Lottie's throat and sputtered out onto her Jabba the Hut chin. My sister heaved a big sigh of relief. But Aunt Lottie didn't miss a beat—she gobbled up the turkey chunk on her chin and then immediately went back to hoovering down the rest of her dinner—like a German Shepherd tearing into raw meat. She only looked up for a moment to ask me if I wanted another beer.

We got all of the plates and tupperware together and said good-by to Aunt Lottie. My brother Mark stopped at the door, and shouted in to her: "Hey, Aunt Lottie, next Thanksgiving we're gonna bring you a milkshake instead."

Visions of Ben

I.

My friend Ben—who never ever wore shoes—rented a house on Great Swamp Pond—he used to swim in the mucky brown water and catch water snakes, hypnotizing them with one hand, pulsing his fingers in the water in front of their eyes and then grabbing them around the throat with the other.

Wild man Ben—had a battered old canoe behind his house— he took me for a ride once when we were both stoned. We paddled up the pond and then onto a stream— that led to a bigger stream—that led to a rapid river. I got scared and para- noid seeing the white water as we approached the river, and I grabbed a shrub root on the bank, trying to stop the canoe. Ben pulled me back and told me to trust him—that it would be a cosmic, other-worldly experience. It was.

II.

Hipster party at Patti and Ruth and Maggie's house in May—the end of my junior year. Crazy Ben—screaming in the back yard and dancing barefoot to a Neil Young song. I was walking out through the doorway of the back porch, and Ben bounded up to me like an excited bear cub and shoved my head through the plate glass window in the door. Shards of glass flew everywhere—a couple got stuck in my face and head. Ben just bellowed his crazy laugh and danced away. Patti, the angelic hipster, took me inside and cleaned up the cuts on my face and put a band-aid on my forehead. Then I went back outside again—and there was Ben—he let out a primordial scream and then he picked up a lawn chair and hurled it at my head like a giant frisbee. The chair whipped over my head and landed on the roof of the house. Ben screamed again, so I ran back inside the house with Patti— we locked ourselves in her bedroom and hung out—with the sound of Ben's savage screams still searing through the night.

III.

My college graduation at the University of Rhode Island—
lined up in hot June sun, listening to the crowd respond to
the names of graduates. The sorority girls all got choruses of
cute celebratory shrieks, and the frat guys got barked
at and had their nicknames hollered out by a lot of other frat
guys. Most everyone else got a couple of lonely claps. When
my name was read off, however, there was a primordial
scream from the top of Davis Hall, where the bell tower was.
Everyone looked up—and there was Ben—wild-haired, barefoot—scaling the outside wall of the bell tower carrying a
large rock—like a stone-age savage. He screamed again and
then started pounding on the bell with his rock—as campus
security rushed to Davis Hall. This was a different kind of
fraternity.

IV.

Grown-up Ben—fifteen years after my college graduation—
Ben is the father of four daughters. We run into Ben and his
family in a rustic campground on the coast of Maine. Sitting
around a campfire with Ben and his two oldest daughters,
thirteen and twelve years old—drinking beer—telling stories—
catching up. I start to wonder if Ben has really settled down—
become responsible—soft—but I watch the wild spark in his
eyes reflect the campfire flame. He tells his daughters he sees
something shiny in the fire— something like a diamond—and
he sticks his hand right into the middle of the fire to get it . . .
It's the second oldest daughter, Diana, who stops him, saying
"No Dad!" and tugs his arm back. She's the responsible one.

Nam Vets on Barstools

Adam and Eve's was a bar in New York City just outside of Washington Square. It was always dark, it had a great juke-box, and pitchers of Pabst Blue Ribbon were three dollars. I was sitting at a table with my friend Steve, waiting to meet Colin and Nancy, who were coming down from New Haven.

Steve was dressed all in black, as usual, and was wearing his round John Lennon sunglasses. I'd known Steve for years, but I still didn't really know all that much about him. He used to be a songwriter and the lead singer in a punk rock band called "Dr. Sahib," a name that Steve had gotten from an article about a vigilante who went around in Chinese prisons late at night and poked out the eyes of convicted murderers and rapists with bicycle spokes. Steve was now a journalist and a late-night disc jockey. I knew that both of his parents had died when he was an adolescent, but I didn't know how. He'd been living with an uncle in Hartford, a quiet man in his forties with sunken eyes.

As we waited for Colin and Nancy, Steve looked around at the people in the bar. "Nam vets on barstools," he said, quot-ing a Dr. Sahib song, "living with the bomb."

Steve was at the jukebox when Colin and Nancy showed up. Colin always advanced into a room like a ham actor. He was a playwright, or at least he was calling himself a playwright. He was wearing a new black suit jacket and a purple scarf. I was reminded of how some people in high school had called him "colon." Nancy walked beside him with her head down, look-ing tired.

Steve's songs played as Colin chattered away, about his lat-est idea for a play, about his latest sexual adventure, about his latest social cause. Colin was involved, among other things, in a protest against mandatory military draft registration. Lou Reed was singing "Heroin" on the jukebox. Steve sat back and stared at his beer. He and Colin had never gotten along.

"The frustrating part of our protest," Colin said, "is that we're fighting for the rights of naïve eighteen year-olds, and a lot of them don't realize that we're trying to help them. The government is putting a real patriotic brainwashing trip on high school kids."

A gravelly voice from the table next to ours broke in: "Fucking spineless weasel. No discipline. No fucking guts." A lean-faced man in a battered army jacket was looking at Colin. One of his eyes looked like it was made out of glass. "What the fuck do you know anyway," he said.

Colin, momentarily stunned, glanced at Steve, then spoke to me, breaking into what sounded like a rehearsed spiel. "Well, here's a patriot. Part of the brainwashing process. The 'I had to go through it, so you should too' mentality." He glanced in the general direction of the next table. "You probably think being in the army straightens kids out, don't you? Does them good?"

"Damn right, it does. Every eighteen-year-old American kid should serve his country for two years. Make'em grow up. Make'em learn something important. Helluva a lot better'n four years of learnin' how to piss and moan in college."
"Oh, learning how to kill somebody makes you grow up?" Colin shot back.

"Watchin' someone die does," said the man with the glass eye. "What the fuck do you know about it anyway."

I was uneasy. I thought he was going to hit Colin with a bottle. Except he didn't have a bottle; he was drinking a pitcher of beer by himself. He had his eyes locked onto Colin's now; he had Colin scared. Talk was no good now.

Steve broke the silence with his calm, monotone voice. "There are only four or five people in the world that I could see myself killing," he said. "And they're all Americans. I wouldn't kill anybody I didn't know."

The man with the glass eye stared at Steve, confused. He seemed to decide that Colin wasn't worth his time any more. The tension was too thick. I got up and went to the jukebox— to change the mood, or at least to avoid getting hit by shattered glass. I put on the Grateful Dead.

When I got back to the table the glass-eyed man was sitting next to Steve, sharing his pitcher with him. They weren't actually talking, but they seemed to be getting along. Colin was standing up; he told me that he had to meet somebody. I sat down next to Steve. The glass-eyed man nodded at me. "Good tune," he said.

Nebraska A&P

Driving cross-country with Jeff, running low on money in Nebraska—with no friends in Nebraska to stop and see and let feed us—Jeff pulls into an A&P supermarket and puts on his big, green winter coat—even though it's March and sixty degrees out. Jeff, with his angelic little kid's face and soft blond curls, has always been able to shoplift without getting caught—because he never looks guilty. He affably says hello to the A&P workers, reading their nametags and calling them by name—Mabel Gaines, Kirk Wiedel—all the while filling his pockets and sleeves with luncheon meat and cans of soup and Chef Boy-R-Dee spaghetti. And then when we get to the dairy aisle, Jeff grabs a couple of cans of Reddi Whip whipped cream and sits down cross-legged on the floor. I sit down next to him, and we hold the cans up- right and suck the nitrous oxide out to get the sixty-second numbing head buzz. And in between nitrous hits Jeff pulls out his harmonica and starts to play an old Neil Young song from Harvest—while sitting on the floor of the dairy section of the A&P. People walking by just smile at him—until one elegantly dressed, middle aged lady in an enormous fur coat stops and scowls at us, making the tsuh sound with her tongue. Then she starts talking to the other customers— about how disgusting we are—but they don't stop and talk to her—they don't want to hear it. So she glares at Jeff and shakes her head. And Jeff looks at the fur coat and says, "Hey, Paulie, have you seen my Yak? I seem to have lost it . . . Oh, there it is!" pointing to the fur coat. And the woman leaves in a huff, presumably to get the store manager, and so we get up. Jeff buys a pack of gum, and says good-by to Mabel Gaines—and we head off, west, to leave Nebraska behind us.

Siren Song

Maggie heard it first; she thought that it was a baby crying. I thought that it was the sound of a cat in heat. But it was too loud to be a cat. Too deep. I leaned out of the window and looked down. I saw blood. And a very fat woman lying on the cement. The inhuman wailing noise was pouring out of her throat. I jerked my head back inside to keep myself from throwing up.

Maggie sat on the window sill and leaned way out to investigate. "Her leg is caught," she told me. "She must have been washing her windows and fell off the ladder. It looks like part of the ladder is going right through her leg."

"Jesus," I said.

"There's a puddle of blood under her head," Maggie went on. "I'm going down to help."

Maggie rushed off. She was able to handle gory situations, for some reason. I stayed at the window, listening to the wail. But I couldn't look down. Instead, I looked across the alley to the apartment behind mine. A woman was watching the bloody scene from an open window. She was topless, her large, bare breasts hanging out of the window. The droning noise kept going on, at the same pitch. I kept staring at the woman's naked breasts. Somehow it reminded me of standing at my father's hospital bed for the last time, years before, listening to the helpless, gurgling wheeze. Instead of watching my father die, I'd stared at the young nurse's legs. And her immaculate white Reebok walking shoes.

Finally the mechanical noise of an ambulance siren joined and then overpowered the scream of the injured fat woman. A crowd of people started to gather soon after the arrival of the ambulance. A crowd of vacant, expressionless faces in a dirty alley, just looking for something interesting.

North Beach

North Beach in San Francisco, halfway through a long, long road trip with Jeff. Haunting the old haunts of the mad beat poets of the '50's. Ferlinghetti's City Lights Bookstore. And next door, Vesuvio's—the bar where Jack Kerouac got crazy drunk so many times. But we couldn't get into Vesuvio's; Jeff didn't have his license with him. And Jeff looked like a little kid, with his long curly blond hair hanging in his eyes. So we had to sit out on the curb on Columbus Avenue and wait for Dean to show up with Jeff's van. And so we sat, and yelled at the Vesuvio's bouncer who wouldn't let Jeff in, and drank the rest of our cheap white wine out of a paper bag—when out of nowhere Ferlinghetti himself came loping up the sidewalk toward us. Old Lawrence Ferlinghetti, in jeans, his workboots tied together and dangling from his neck, smiling at us with the brightest flashing blue eyes in the world. Jeff said, "Hi Lawrence, how's it going?" and he just smiled and nodded and sat down on the curb with us. And he listened to us complain about the bouncer at Vesuvio's, and about the problems with the starter in Jeff's van, and he sat with us and listened and nodded with kind understanding eyes for ten minutes or so, and then he got up and shook our hands, and nodded, and disappeared in City Lights. He had never said a word to us.

Later, in a bar called Gulliver's, still on Columbus Avenue, we sat with Dean and John McCarron, listening to a blond tough-girl blues singer who looked like Jodie Foster, ripping out bruising guitar licks. Dean had bought a few ounces of psilocybin mushrooms and he just dumped them on the table and we ate them like hors d'oeuvres. Hallucinogenic mushrooms and Budweiser. And a crunching blues band. And Dean pulled out his harmonica and started playing with the band. And as the mushrooms kicked in we were all pounding out the rhythm on the table, and I could have sworn I saw Ferlinghetti smiling in through the window from Columbus Ave. And all of a sudden Dean put down his harmonica and started scribbling out a poem on a napkin. But he was still playing the same song.

Teacher's Pet

I was teaching Title One reading at the Thomas Edison Middle School in Boston. I had gotten the job because the original Title One reading teacher had been poisoned by one of her students. Some seventh or eighth grader had put copy machine fluid into her coffee, and when she got out of the hospital she decided that she didn't want her job back for some reason.

Title One was a reading program for kids who had problems with reading. I had between six and ten students each period, seventh and eighth graders who had second and third grade reading levels. I found that they did better when they were reading about things that interested them: sports, or rap musicians, or anything remotely relating to sex.

My best student was a fifteen-year-old boy named Calvin. He was a quick-witted and very enterprising young man. He was a ball boy for the Boston Celtics. And he also had a second job—in sales. One day Calvin tried to sell me a handgun. I could tell that he had a real sense of pride in his work as he showed me the gun. It was a very nice gun. I didn't buy it, but I knew right then that Calvin was going to pass my class. I never told the school administrators about the gun; Calvin had trusted me. That was important. And I let him know that I wasn't happy about his being involved with guns; he knew that I was worried about him.

In June, everyone made a really big deal over graduation— from this middle school. Graduating eighth graders rented tuxedoes and bought elegant gowns; parents rented limousines for the occasion—all of this because it was assumed that most of these kids would never make it through high school. So this was their big day—their crowning achievement.

Calvin sought me out during graduation. He handed me a brown paper grocery bag—a "thank you" present, he called it. It was a VCR videotape. "It's a bootleg porno video," Calvin told me. "It's my new line of work."

"Porno?" I asked.

Calvin shrugged. "It's what I do," he said. "I'm not selling guns no more." I nodded and thanked him. "It's called 'The Pink Lagoon,'" he said. "It's my top seller with the white folks." He smiled. "Lotta necked blond people runnin' around on an island."

I asked him where he'd be going to high school in the fall, and he shrugged and looked away. "Not sure," he said. He had to survive. We both knew that survival would be a more difficult for him—that he'd most likely die before I would. A year of life in the inner city is equal to about two or three suburban years. Kind of like dog years. In a dog-eat-dog world.

On the Outskirts of Reno

Reno, Nevada—just passing through—riding across the country with Jeff, ultimately to find Dean and Steve in San Francisco. It's three in the morning and we're almost out of gas—we stop at a gas station lit by a bright orange fluorescent light sign announcing "GAS / GAMBLING / BAR." Jeff fills the tank and we go in to pay. The inside of the gas station is a shabby-looking bar with a juke box blaring country music— "Drivin' My Life Away"—and four grubby tough guys with beards sitting at a table with one drunk woman with scads of eye make-up, playing mumbly peg with a big hunting knife. One of the grubby tough guys is the bartender/cashier—but he doesn't get up—or even look at us.

Jeff calls over to him from the counter, asking for a couple of beers—and the bartender doesn't answer. Jeff shrugs and goes to the juke box, and l move over to the bartender's table and ask again for beer. No response. And then one of the others says: "That yer girlfriend over there at the juke box? He has such purty hair." All of a sudden I feel like Jack Nicholson in the Texas diner with Dennis Hopper in Easy Rider —right before he's beaten to death. Jeff plays an electric Neil Young song on the juke box— "Hey Hey, My My." The grubby tough guys don't like it. One guy, whose head looks like an ampu-tated arm, shouts out, "Hey what the hell's this crap?" and he pulls the hunting knife out of the table. I look up at Jeff—he swings his head toward the door. I follow him to the car and get in.

"Well, that sucked," I say, as Jeff starts up the car.

"I don't know," Jeff says with his good-natured smile, "at least they let us have free gas." And he speeds away, back into the fluorescent Nevada night.

Poverello's

So there's this place in Missoula, Montana, that serves free meals once a day—to hobos and vagrants and stuff—It's called Poverello's. Cal and I used to go there almost every day that summer, and we made a lot of really scruffy friends. There was a regular there that we nicknamed Owlsley—because he seemed to have done more acid than anyone alive, and we figured that maybe he'd actually invented acid. And there was another guy named Jim that always wore a yellow construction helmet, and he looked like Lee Marvin in the movie Cat Balou. Jim never ever talked—not even once for like two months.

And then one day I was sitting next to Jim at dinner—it was lasagna night—with tapioca pudding for desert. And Owsley was really strung out—quivering—and he was frantically searching his pockets, and searching the table for something—and as Owlsley was looking around the table, he started moving things, and by chance he moved Jim's tapioca pudding. And Jim went nuts. He picked up a fork and waved it over his head, and then he leaned towards Owlsly with it, as if he were going to jab Owlsly in the neck. He still didn't actually talk, but he started to whine, and then bay like a coyote—louder and louder—at a higher and higher pitch. And strung-out Owlsley just started to laugh, and he kept saying, "Calm down, Jim. I'm not gonna take your goddam pudding." And then they both started to convulse—and Jim fell off his chair—and hit the floor like a sandbag. Owlsley just kept laughing and convulsing—and then he grabbed Jim's tapioca pudding and ran out the front door with it.

The old guy sitting on the other side of me shook his head. "There's always trouble on tapioca pudding night," he said.

Elegant Glasses

Jeff bought elegant cocktail glasses at a garage sale, four for a quarter—and he was very excited about them. He liked to use them to make vodka tonics in—his favorite drink—and he'd put in cut up limes and cucumber spears, and sometimes slices of pineapple or mango, to make them look even more elegant. He'd wear his same old crumpled white button-down shirt and ripped up jeans and his Neil Young suede vest—but holding an exotic drink in his elegant cocktail glass, he said he felt like F. Scott Fitzgerald.

One night our friends Annie and Martha and Ruth had invited us to a party. It was a "mushroom party." They'd just bought a couple pounds of "psychedelic" psilocybin mushrooms, and they went on a cooking frenzy with them. They made a psychedelic mushroom and eggplant casserole, a psychedelic mushroom salad, and psychedelic mushroom granola oatmeal cookies. For appetizers, they had stuffed psychedelic mushrooms. We brought vodka and Jeff's elgant cocktail glasses. Annie put psychedelic mushrooms in her vodka tonic, but Jeff said that was overdoing it.

After a couple hours of dinner and pleasant hallucinations, Jeff said he needed to get out. He wanted to go for a drive down one of the private oceanside roads on the shore where the millionaires lived. So I went with him. We went to a road on the other side of town, clearly marked: Private Drive—no trespassing. We drove down the private road slowly, and casually observed the mansions and the ocean backdrop through a psychedelic haze, all the while drinking festive vodka tonics in elegant cocktail glasses. Within minutes a police car was behind us with blue lights flashing. An enormous cop appeared at Jeff's door, sneering down, looking like an over-inflated Sylvester Stallone. He hated college kids, we could tell. He took Jeff's license and registration. Then he saw our drinks. "What the hell's that?" he snapped. Jeff smiled. "Exotic fruit drinks in elegant glasses," he said. "Why mine even has cut up cucumbers and mango slices in it, to add a festive

88

holiday feel." The cop was taken aback; he'd obviously been expecting to find beer. "Wait here," he snarled.

He kept us waiting for what must have been an hour, supposedly checking Jeff's registration. I figure he was just trying to make us nervous—to make us sweat. But we were having a blast just hallucinating, thrilled and delighted watching the pretty blue lights from the police car flash around on the mansions and the rocky ocean shore like a kaleidoscope, turning the coastline into a gigantic, shimmering blue jello mold. "This is kind of like a Pink Floyd concert," Jeff said.

Finally the cop turned off the flashing light and brought Jeff his registration back. "You're all set," he said. "No citation this time. Just stay away from this street." Jeff thanked him, and then called him back as he was turning away. He said, "Hey, could you do us a favor?"

"What," the big cop said.

"Could you just turn on that flashing blue light for just one more minute," Jeff asked. "That was wicked cool."

Fishing with Ben

Ben had told me that I could make some fast money fishing with him for a few days on one of the commercial fishing boats he worked on out of Newport. I really needed money. Just show up, he told me over the phone. So I did.

After a long night of cheap red Gallo wine, drunken screaming to Ben's old Bob Dylan tapes, and passing out on the kitchen floor, he woke me up at four in the morning to go to work. "Fuck you," I said, and rolled over. Ben laughed and yanked me to my feet by the shirt collar. Then he shoved a cup of industrial strength coffee into my face.

A half-hour later we were on the dock in Newport harbor, waiting for the foreman with five or six semi-conscious drunks looking for work. One guy, who looked like TomWaits, was reading Nietzsche, with a pint of Jim Beam bourbon resting on his lap. Then the foreman showed up—a crusty thug right out of "Good Fellas." Ben talked to him for a minute. "You're all set," Ben told me. "We need as many guys as possible—we're pulling up the leader nets today." "Oh." "They been out there a while."

They gave me a raincoat, but I was the only one there without my own boots—so I had to slosh around the deck in my sneakers. The boat was smaller than I had figured, maybe fifty feet—just a big, loud engine spewing out soot and a deep plastic tub to throw fish into. I felt sick right away.

The first line of net that we pulled in had a dead hammerhead shark caught in it. Long dead. Rotting. It was stuck in the net right over my head. Ben gave me a jackknife to cut it free. Instead, it fell apart, like gelatin, splattering onto my face. Tom Waits and the foreman both laughed hard; they were both missing quite a few teeth.

The main catch of the day was a huge load of bonitos, big blue-green mackerels that people said tasted like tuna—and the foreman seemed happy with the catch. More fish were tangled in the nets and had to be cut loose. Tom Waitts sliced off the tip of his thumb and blood ran down his arm. I went nuts and ran around to everyone on the boat, screaming that he'd cut the tip of his thumb off, but no one seemed to care. He poured some Jim Beam over it, took a swig, and tied a ripped piece of his flannel shirt around the thumb. No big deal.

By ten o'clock we had all the fish our boat could hold, so we started back. Ben did a wild dance, sloshing around the back of the boat in his big rubber boots. Most of the guys were trying to catch the seagulls who were after our bonitos. One guy dove for a seagull and slid off the boat into the water. Ben grabbed a bonito and cut it up with his jackknife; then he wrapped it in a piece of tin foil and threw it onto the engine of the boat. Twenty minutes later, we were eating the sweetest, most tender fish I'd ever tasted. Ben grabbed my shoulders and started to scream: "A half-hour ago that fish was alive! Now you're a part of the food chain, dude!"

We docked and unloaded the bonitos in big plastic garbage cans, and brought them into an ice house on the dock. Then I went to get my pay. The foreman wouldn't pay me—the crusty "Good Fellas" thug; he smiled and said he didn't know who I was. Ben came in carrying a bonito and smacked the foreman hard on the side of the head with it. "Pay my friend," he yelled, and then smacked him on the head again. The foreman jumped Ben, and the two of them wrestled around on the slimy wooden floor, until Ben finally pinned him. "It's all part of the ritual," Ben told me, wiping fish crud off his face. "Swell," I said. The foreman paid me. Fifty dollars, in cash. Ben slapped me on the back, smiled and said, "Yeah, well, I know things may seem a little rough now, but it'll go better tomorrow." "Fuck you," I said. Ben smiled knowingly. "You'll be back," he said.

On the way home we stopped and picked up a couple gallons of cheap Gallo wine. But this time we got white wine—to go with the fresh bonito that Ben had snuck into his car.

The End of the World

I was in a bar on Comm. Ave. called "Streets," with my friends Steve and Jack. The entire bar was painted black: the walls, the floor, the bar—even the windows were painted black. The band was playing loud, synthesized new wave music and trying to make themselves appear machine-like. All wearing the same mirror sunglasses. Artificial drum- beat. Monotone singing. The people dancing hopped and lurched mechanically—up and down, back and forth. Most of the people there were girls dancing alone. I went up to one girl dancing alone who looked like Debbie Harry, the lead singer of the rock group Blondie. Sleepy, strung-out eyes, bright red lipstick, and shaggy blond bangs falling diagonally over one eye. I started dancing with her. She smiled vacantly at me. She was wasted.

After a couple of songs, the girl fell into my arms exhausted. Lifeless. I tried to guess what she was on. Probably a combination, I figured, but amyl nitrate was probably involved.
"You're beautiful," I told her. "You look like Blondie." She smiled and kissed me.
" Where were you sitting? Do you remember?" The girl pointed, and I led her to the table. There was one other girl alone at the table, with long black hair and sharp, dark eyes.

I found out that the blonde's name was Anita. The dark- haired girl, who was dressed all in black, told me that she was a witch.
"That's good, because you look like a witch," I told her.
Anita kept spinning her head back and forth, and the witch began telling me that the world was going to end that night.
"The thirteenth, man," she told me. "It's written. At ten-thirty." She looked at her watch. "Five more hours,"
she said.
"It's after ten-thirty now," I told her.
The witch laughed, throwing her head back. "Yeah, their clocks, man. Their time."
"Did you guys do acid tonight?" I asked the witch.
"Fuck you," she said.
Anita stood up, wavering. She looked pale.
"Um goin' bathroom," she blurted out, and then stumbled off.

"I think she might be sick," I said, and the witch laughed. I asked the witch if she was into Ozzy Osborne, and she got really mad. She narrowed her eyes into an evil glare, and she started to vomit, looking just like Linda Blair in The Exorcist. I ducked out of the way, and then I just started running. I bombed through the door and just kept moving. There was another bar a few blocks away called the El Phoenix; I knew that I'd be safe there.

Back then almost every night it seemed as if the world was going to end. I just didn't want to be listening to bad music, and being   vomited on by a witch when it ended.

Side Show

Once when I was 18, and a little bit drunk, I went to a carnival side show with my rowdy friends Bob and Missaiko. The carnival was out in the lot behind the old shopping center on the outskirts of Manchester, CT. Outside the entrance to the side show tent there was a sandwich board sign announcing the featured performers: "The Amazing Rubber Lady" and "The Amazon Giant."

We paid five dollars to a shyster pitchman in a very loud plaid sportcoat and headed in. The Amazon Giant went on first—she was a very large Black woman, maybe six foot eight, with an enormous head. The shyster pitchman introduced her as "the largest woman on Earth." Her act was that she put very long, sharp objects up her nose. She started with a large nail, then she slid a spike up her nostril, and then a Phillips head screwdriver. It seemed too easy. When she pulled out a foot-long ice-pick, I knew it had to be rigged.

"That's so fake," I shouted out. "That's just a theatre prop." The Amazon Giant glared at me. "Would someone from the audience like to check the ice-pick?" she asked.

"You bet your ass," I snapped, and I hopped up on the rickety stage. She handed me the ice-pick. I looked for the trick release button—I couldn't find one.

"Satisfied?" she grunted. I figured that there must have been some sort of automatic release in the blade.

"Observe!" I shouted to the audience. I placed the tip of the ice-pick into my own nostril and gave the handle a shove. Immediately there was a sharp, stinging pain, and blood began to flow out of my nose. I screamed like a little kid: "Ow, ow, ow, ow, ow!" Without flinching, the Amazon Giant grabbed the ice-pick out of my hand and quickly shoved it up her own nose all the way to the handle.

A loud woman in the back of the crowd said, "Oh, he's just part of the act." I started to scream at her: "Screw you, lady, I'm BLEED-ING goddammit," and I started to storm off the stage. The Amazon Giant grabbed me by the collar with one hand, as if I were a puppy. To calm me down the shyster pitchman told me that I could view the Amazing Rubber Lady inside of her box for free—normally you had to pay an extra five dollars—so I was happy.

It turned out "The Amazing Rubber Lady" was a let down. She was just a really skinny, sickly-looking woman who scrunched herself into a short foot-locker while the shyster pitchman slid flimsy swords into pre-measured slots. She looked as if she were in pain. It was sad. But the Amazon Giant—she was REAL. After her bit was over, she just disappeared. And I didn't try to find her. Some things just aren't meant to be understood by mere mortals.

Paul Rogalus teaches film and writing at Plymouth State University, in New Hampshire. His full-length play Crawling From the Wreckage was produced in New York City by the American Theatre of Actors, and his one act plays have been produced in New York, Chicago, and Boston.

He has two chapbooks of micro-stories: "Meat Sculptures" (Green Bean Press), and "Electrified Skeletons"
(Medulla Review Publishing).

www.ingramcontent.com/pod-product-compliance
Lightning Source LLC
Chambersburg PA
CBHW071142250626
47159CB00006B/2265